Alien & Possum
Hanging Out

by **Tony Johnston**

pictures by **Tony DiTerlizzi**

Aladdin Paperbacks
New York   London   Toronto   Sydney   Singapore

For the folks of Brasstown, North Carolina,
possum capital of the United States of America—T. J.

For Harry Rountree—I couldn't have painted Possum
without you.—T. D.

First Aladdin Paperbacks edition May 2003
Text copyright © 2002 Johnston Family Trust
Illustrations copyright © 2002 by Tony DiTerlizzi

ALADDIN PAPERBACKS
An imprint of Simon & Schuster Children's Publishing Division
1230 Avenue of the Americas, New York, NY 10020

Cover design by Greg Stadnyk and Lisa Vega
Book design by Greg Stadnyk
The text of this book was set in Bembo.
Printed in Mexico
2 4 6 8 10 9 7 5 3 1

Also available in a Simon and Schuster Books for Young Readers hardcover edition.
The Library of Congress has cataloged the hardcover edition as follows:
Johnston, Tony, 1942–
Alien and Possum hanging out / Tony Johnston, Tony DiTerlizzi—1st ed
p. cm.
Summary: Two good friends, Possum and Alien, spend time together celebrating their birthdays, discovering their uniqueness,
and hanging out together in a tree.
ISBN 0-689-83836-0 (hc)
[1. Opossums—Fiction. 2. Extraterrestrial beings—Fiction. 3. Friendship—Fiction.] I. DiTerlizzi, Tony. II. Title.
PZ7.J6478 Alf 2002
[Emma]—dc21
00-052233

ISBN 0-689-85771-3 (Aladdin pbk.)

Contents

One of a Kind

In the woods where Possum lived, there were many possums and many foxes and many beetles, all alike. Even the trees were of the same kind, wearing their same bark all year long.

Alien felt forlorn.

"You look forlorn," said Possum.

"I am," said Alien sadly. *Crank, Crink, Croooooonk!*

"But why?" asked Possum.
"We are having fun."

"You are," said Alien. "I am not."

"What?" asked Possum.

"There are many possums, Possum," said Alien. "There are many foxes. There are many beetles, all alike. And trees wearing their same bark."

"That is true," said Possum.

"I do not look like anyone else," moped Alien.

"True," said Possum.

"I do not sound like anyone else," moaned Alien.

"True," said Possum.

Alien touched its sleek, colorful sides.

"I do not *feel* like anyone else," Alien wailed.

Possum patted Alien's sleek, colorful sides. They felt sleek. They felt colorful.

"True," said Possum. "What is your point?"

Alien howled, "I AM ALONE!"

Possum's heart squeezed tight.
He thought about that.

While he thought, Alien wept. First tear
by tear, then in a rushing gush, Alien
had a crying fit. Soon its sleek, colorful
sides were wet.

"Stop crying," said Possum.

"Why should I?" asked Alien.

"Because," Possum shouted,
"YOU ARE ONE OF A KIND!"

"Is that good?" Alien sniffled.

"It is the best," said Possum.

"Is that *really* good?" Alien snuffled.

"It is the best of the best," said Possum.

Alien pepped up.

"Oooh," it said. "OOOOOOOOOH!"

Possum wiped Alien's tears with a cloth,
so that Alien's joints would not rust.

Alien beamed. It gleamed.
It screamed over and over,
"I AM ONE OF A KIND!"

Possum wiped slow. And slower.
He looked glum. And glummer.

"What is wrong, Possum?" asked Alien.

"There are trillions of possums," said Possum. "There are kazillions of possums. There are kerbillions of possums. There are skadillions of possums. I AM LIKE EVERYONE ELSE IN THE WHOLE WIDE WORLD!"

Possum wept up a sadness storm.

"Possum?" said Alien.

Possum said, "I am too sad to talk."

Alien said, "Well, I am not. There are
trillions and kazillions and kerbillions
and skadillions of possums. But there is
only one possum like you."

"Oooh," said Possum behind his tears. "OOOOOOOOOOH!" Possum grinned. "Well, why did you take so long to say that?" he asked. "Now my fur is wet."

"Do not worry," said Alien. "I will dry it."

And it did.

Happy Birthdays

Possum was happy. It was his birthday.
"Hooray! Hooray!" Possum shouted.

Skrink! Skronk! Skreek! Alien woke up.
"Who-what?" it shrieked.

"Hooray!" Possum danced.
"It is my birthday!"

"What is that?" asked Alien.

Possum looked surprised. He blinked his eyes. "It is the day I was born," he said. "The day I first knew the world. We must have a party for me."

Alien looked surprised. It swirled its eyes.

"What is a party?" asked Alien.

"A highly festive time," said Possum, "in which you eat too much frosting and sing the birthday song and dance all over the place."

"Even on the table?" asked Alien hopefully.

"Even on the table," said Possum.

Possum and Alien made decorations for Possum's birthday party.

Alien made pretty paper chains.

It said, "I do not have a birthday." Its voice got low and slow.

Possum was so amazed, he plopped
down on the floor.

He said, "You *must* have a birthday.
Everyone does."

Alien said, "I am sad to say that I do not."

Possum sat on the floor for a long time, thinking.

He made a noise like lots of bees, *"Hmmmmmmmmm."*

He made a sound like a breeze in trees, *"Hmmmmmmmmm."*

He made a wheeze like electric knees, *"Hmmmmmmmmm."*

At last Possum said,
"We will choose you a birthday, Alien."

"Goody!" cried Alien.

Alien got excited. It ran all over the place. *Dit-dit-dit-dit-dit-dit-dit.*

"A birthday! A birthday!" Alien cronked and creaked. "When–when–*when*?"

"The day your spaceship came. The day you first knew the world," Possum said.

"But *when-when-when*?" asked Alien.

"Two weeks ago," said Possum.

"Oh," said Alien. "I am old."

"We must have two parties," Possum said. "Two at the same time—even though your birthday has gone. We will invite everyone."

Possum invited some animals he knew.

He didn't invite just any fox, but Fox.

He didn't invite just any woodpecker,
but Woodpecker.

He didn't invite just any beetles, but the
Beetle Boys, who lived in a nice, rotten
stump.

They baked two cakes. They put
sparklers on them. Because sparklers
look like fizzy stars.

Alien and Possum decorated for their
birthdays. They swooped pretty paper
chains all over for Possum. They flooped
doodads of foil everywhere for Alien.

Fox and Woodpecker and the Beetle Boys arrived. With presents.

They said "Happy birthdays" to Alien and Possum.

Everyone had a highly festive time.

They ate too much frosting. They
sang—and creaked—the birthday song.
They danced all over the place—
even on the table.

Hanging Out

Sometimes Possum went
out by day. He enjoyed the clouds.
He enjoyed the leaves. He enjoyed the
butterflies.

One day Possum was hanging
upside down from a branch.

Dit-dit-dit. Alien came along.

"What are you doing, Possum?"
asked Alien.

"I am hanging upside down from a branch," Possum answered.

"Oh," said Alien. "What for?"

"For fun," said Possum. "There is nothing more fun than hanging upside down from a good high branch."

"There isn't?" asked Alien.

"No, there isn't," said Possum.
"The world looks lovely from here.
It makes me feel new. Come and see."

Alien crept up the tree trunk. *Dit-dit-dit.*
It turned itself over. *Dit-dit-dit.*

It crawled out on the branch.
Zip-zip-zip. Wires spronged from its gears.

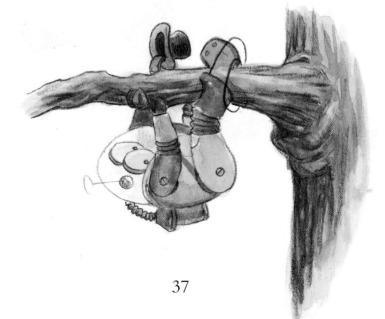

Then Alien hung next to Possum,
upside down.

Electricity rushed to Alien's head.
Everything was a big blur.

"How does the world look now, Alien?"
asked Possum.

"It is a big blur," Alien said.

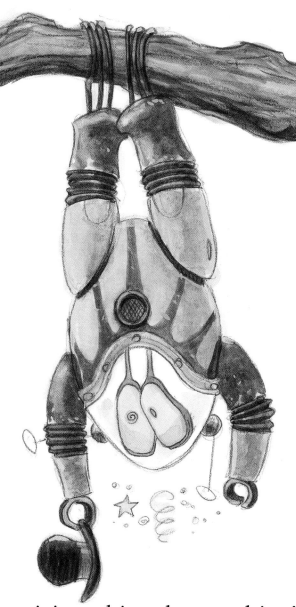

Electricity whizzed around in Alien's head. Alien got dizzy.

It was not fun.

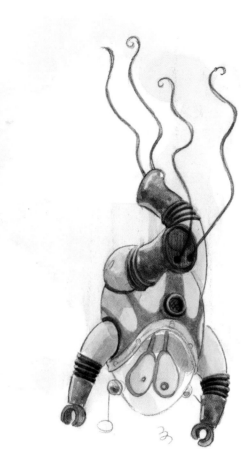

"Do you feel new now, Alien?" asked Possum.

"I feel dizzy now," said Alien. "So dizzy I could drop."

CRONK! Alien dropped to the ground.

BONK! Alien landed on its head.

"Alien!" screeched Possum.

He rushed to his friend.

"Are you all right?" asked Possum. "You look stiff."

"I *am* stiff, Possum," said Alien. "I am metal. Also, I am bonked."

Possum set Alien rightside up. He dusted Alien off.

"There, Alien," said Possum, "you are rightside up again."

Possum said, "Possums belong in trees. Aliens do not. I am sorry you fell."

"I know that," said Alien.

"I need a little more hanging time,"
Possum said. "I am going back to my
branch."

"But what about me?" sighed Alien.
"I will be all alone."

"You will not be alone," Possum said.
"I will talk to you the whole time."

Possum hung upside down from the
branch. He talked to Alien.

Alien did not listen.

Dit-dit-dit. Alien crept up the tree trunk.

Alien crawled out on the branch.
Dit-dit-dit.

Then Alien hung next to Possum,
rightside up.

"I am glad you are here," said Possum.

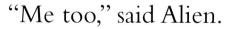

"Me too," said Alien.

Alien and Possum hung out on the branch a long time. They enjoyed the view quietly.

Clouds floated by. Leaves fluttered
down. Butterflies flittered past. At last
Alien said, "The world looks lovely
from here."

"Yes, it does," said Possum.